On the Night
of the Comet

To Kathy Stinson and Peter Carver
—*L.C.*

To my sister, Carol, with love
—*L.E.W.*

National Library of Canada Cataloguing in Publication Data

Coakley, Lena, 1967-
On the night of the comet / Lena Coakley ; Leslie Elizabeth Watts, illustrator.

ISBN 1-55143-287-0

I. Watts, Leslie Elizabeth, 1961- II. Title.

PS8605.O234O5 2004   jC813'.6   C2004-902450-7

First published in the United States 2004
Library of Congress Control Number: 2004105776

Summary: A grieving boy is given another chance to say goodbye when three great cats show up on his doorstep.

Orca Book Publishers gratefully acknowledges the support for its publishing programs provided by the following agencies: the Government of Canada through the Book Publishing Industry Development Program (BPIDP), the Canada Council for the Arts, and the British Columbia Arts Council.

Typesetting and cover design by Lynn O'Rourke
Printed and bound in China

Orca Book Publishers
Box 5626 Stn. B
Victoria, BC Canada
V8R 6S4

Orca Book Publishers
PO Box 468
Custer, WA   USA
98240-0468

08 07 06 05 04 • 5 4 3 2 1

On the Night of the Comet

Story by Lena Coakley

Illustrations by Leslie Elizabeth Watts

ORCA BOOK PUBLISHERS

On the night of the comet, Peter couldn't sleep. A question ran around and around in his head like a cat chasing its tail.

So he was awake when the Persian kitten climbed up on his chest and said, "Scratch me under the chin—also, there are some tigers at the door."

Peter got up in the night, walked past the big empty bedroom, down the stairs and past his father on the couch. He opened the door. Outside it was as bright as noon. Two tigers and a great white snow leopard sat on the stoop.

"Welcome to my house," said the Persian kitten. "This is my boy. He will pet us and give us cream."

The white cat's tail was twice as long as her body. "Thank you," she said. "We have far to go. We are on our way to see the Great Cat. On the night of the comet, when all cats can speak, we ask him our questions."

"I have a question," said Peter.
"It's too far for kittens," the Snow Leopard said.
"We're not kittens," said the Persian kitten.

In the kitchen, Peter drank his cream
from a bowl, just like the cats.

"Shouldn't we be going?" said Peter. But the tigers were peering over the back of the couch where Peter's father snored.

"He looks delicious," they said.

"He isn't," said Peter.

"He looks sad," said the Snow Leopard.

The tigers climbed the stairs. "You can't go in there,"
Peter said, but the tigers went into the big empty bedroom.
"What's wrong with these trees?" they asked.
"Those are plants," said Peter. "No one waters them now."
"Why is this place so empty?"
"My mother and father slept here, but now everything
has changed."

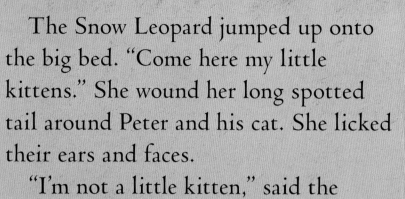

The Snow Leopard jumped up onto the big bed. "Come here my little kittens." She wound her long spotted tail around Peter and his cat. She licked their ears and faces.

"I'm not a little kitten," said the Persian kitten. "I'm a lion."

"So am I," Peter murmured. "We'll stay for just a minute, then we'll go to see...the...Great...Cat." Peter drifted off to sleep.

When Peter awoke, the tigers were nibbling his toes. They tried to speak but could only growl.

"The night of the comet is almost over," said the Snow Leopard. "They are forgetting themselves."

The tigers chased the Snow Leopard's long tail the way a cat chases a string. She led them out of the bedroom and all over the house. Around and around the couch they ran, while Peter's father slept.

"Open the door," the Snow Leopard said. She lured the tigers outside and shut the door with her nose.

"Now I will have to run all the way to the mountains," she told Peter.

Peter looked out of the window. "It's too far for me, isn't it?"

"I will bring the Great Cat your question. Perhaps I will return someday to bring you the answer."

The Persian kitten said, "Ask him: why am I such a small lion?"

Peter said, "Ask him: why do people have to go away? Why can't things stay the same?"

Peter opened up the front door carefully for the Snow Leopard, but the tigers were nowhere to be seen. "Don't go," he whispered. "Stay here with me."

"Perhaps I would forget myself and eat you up."

"You wouldn't," said Peter.

"I wouldn't," she said. And then she was gone.

"Can't sleep?" said Peter's father.
"No."
"Me neither."

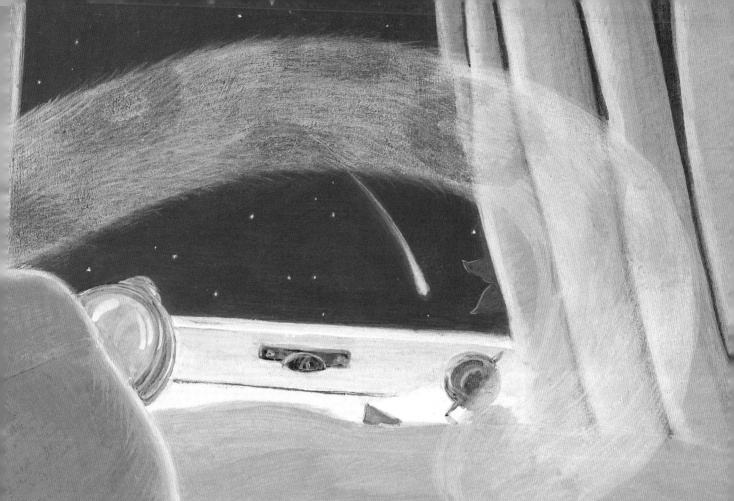

Peter's father took him up to bed and tucked him in. The Persian kitten purred under his chin. Only Peter heard him whisper, "Maybe I could be a kitten if that's what my boy wanted." Outside Peter's window, the comet touched the horizon.

"Dad, I had a dream about a big cat with soft, white fur."

Peter's father said, "I had a dream that tigers were sniffing me."

"In my dream," said Peter, "I forgot to say goodbye. Do you think that if I said it now, she would hear me?"

"Try it," said his father.

Peter looked out of his window.

"Goodbye," he whispered.